The CURSE of EINSTEIN'S PENCIL

written and illustrated by

Deborah Zemke

PUFFIN BOOKS

JUDITH ROSE EINSTEIN

PUFFIN BOOKS
An imprint of Penguin Random House LLC
375 Hudson Street
New York, New York 10014

First published in the United States of America by Dial Books for Young Readers, 2017.
Published by Puffin Books, an imprint of Penguin Random House LLC, 2017

THE LIBRARY OF CONGRESS HAS CATALOGED THE DIAL BOOKS FOR YOUNG READERS EDITION AS FOLLOWS:
Names: Zemke, Deborah.
Title: The curse of Einstein's pencil / Deborah Zemke.
Description: New York : Dial Books for Young Readers, 2017. | Series: Bea Garcia | Summary: "Bea Garcia wants to impress her brainy new friend by excelling at the geography contest, but her talents lie elsewhere and she learns that the best way to make friends is by being herself."— Provided by publisher.
Identifiers: LCCN 2016038938 | ISBN 9780803741553 (hardcover)
Subjects: | CYAC: Friendship—Fiction. | Identity—Fiction. | Drawing—Fiction. | Hispanic Americans—Fiction.
Classification: LCC PZ7.Z423 Cu 2017 | DDC [Fic]—dc23 LC record available at https://lccn.loc.gov/2016038938

Puffin Books ISBN 9780147513137

Printed in the United States of America

1 3 5 7 9 10 8 6 4 2

To John.

Here we are, flying 24,901 miles around the world. . . .

—D.Z.

Chapter 1

MY MAGIC PENCIL

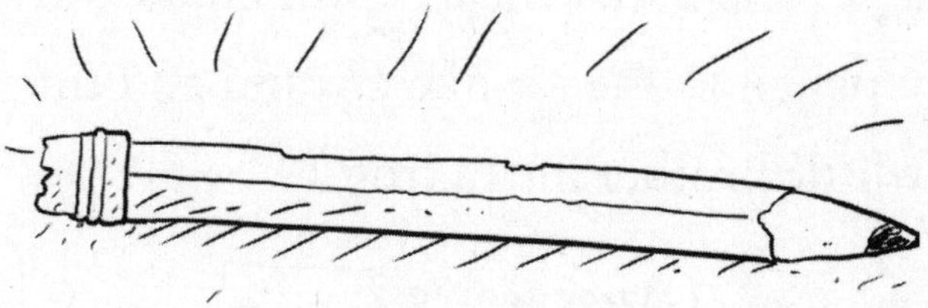

This is my pencil. It may not look magic, but it is. Mrs. Grogan said so. She told the whole class.

Mrs. Grogan didn't mean fairy-tale magic. She didn't mean that I could wave my pencil in the air like a wand and turn my little brother into a frog.

She meant drawing magic, that I could turn my brother into a frog in a picture.

But wouldn't it be fun if I really could turn him into a frog? He would be good at jump rope and basketball.

It would be easy for him to get second helpings of dessert. Of course, if my brother was a frog, his favorite dessert would be fly pie. Yuck.

Anyway, Mrs. Grogan wasn't talking about pictures of frogs. She was talking about this picture that I drew of Mount Everest, the highest place on Earth.

Bea is an artist!

Ignore that monster on top. That's Bert. I wish I'd never drawn him.

This is me, Bea Garcia.

Just kidding! I'm not really a movie star.

But I really am an artist.

I draw pictures of everything, especially my dog, Sophie. And flowers and stars and kangaroos and birds and EVERYTHING.

I draw pictures of what really happens. This is when I turned my little brother into a frog by painting him green.

My brother's name is Pablo, but I call him the Big Pest because he really is one.

I draw pictures of what I WISH would happen. This is me flying around the world to visit my first and only best friend, Yvonne, who moved 10,000 miles away to Australia.

Sometimes I draw pictures of things that could only happen in pictures. Here we are playing with Yvonne's pet kangaroo. I WISH!

Here I really am in my backyard, wishing Yvonne had never moved away.

When I'm drawing, sometimes it seems like the pictures just hop out of my brain and onto the paper.

It's almost like the pencil is drawing the picture all by itself! Like real magic. I know it isn't real, but it feels like it is.

This is the book that I draw in, the book I take everywhere and draw pictures of everything in.

I draw when I'm sitting in the crabapple tree in my backyard . . .

and in bed when I should be sleeping.

I draw in my book when I'm riding on the bus and . . .

at recess when everyone else is playing.

I even draw in class when I'm supposed to be paying attention. Like right now in math.

Mrs. Grogan doesn't think my pencil is very magical in math.

Beatrice Holmes Garcia!
It's time for math, not doodling!

Mrs. Grogan only calls me Beatrice when I've done something wrong. Otherwise she calls me Bea like everybody else. Except Einstein. Einstein ALWAYS calls me Beatrice. Not that Einstein.

Good morning,
Beatrice.

This one. Judith Einstein.

She's the girl who sits next to me in Mrs. Grogan's class.

She's the girl with her hand up, who answers every question, even in math and science and spelling and Top Ten Geography and reading comprehension skills.

Einstein answers all the questions in the universe before Mrs. Grogan even asks. I feel smarter just sitting next to her!

This is Einstein's pencil. See how the eraser has never been used? That's because Einstein never makes mistakes.

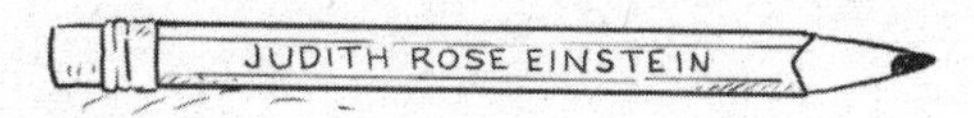

She's the smartest girl in Emily Dickinson School. She's the smartest girl in the universe.

And my almost-friend. Almost.

Chapter 2

BETWEEN A GENIUS AND A MONSTER

Here we are, sitting together on the bus going to school. Einstein and me and my little brother. The Big Pest is pretending that he's a monster, but you can't be a monster if you're a scaredy-cat. Which he definitely is.

Luckily, Einstein doesn't care about him. She's too busy reading. Einstein is always reading. She doesn't talk much outside of class, and I don't always understand what she does say. Here's the first thing she ever said to me.

She said that after Mrs. Grogan told the whole class that my pencil was magic, so I'm pretty sure it meant that Einstein liked my pictures.

I asked my dad what the word *inaccurate* meant and he told me:

Then he helped me to look up *inaccurate*, and I saw that he was right—it meant wrong.

It didn't mean that I'd done something wrong. It meant *NOT CORRECT*. So I'm still not 100 percent sure what Einstein meant, but now I know how to spell *inaccurate* if it ever comes up in a Top Ten Spelling Bee.

I WISH!!

I'm not really a Spelling Bee Superstar. Maybe I would be better at spelling if you could draw pictures of words like this:

I'd be better at everything if I could draw all my answers. Here's the first president of the United States!

Anyway, I know exactly what the second thing that Einstein ever said to me meant.

Here's how I felt when she said that.

Shining high, like a star. Just Einstein and me soaring across the universe. Star Mates!

I WISH!

Ignore that monster on the bus reaching for my book. That's Bert. Yes, the Bert I drew on top of Mount Everest.

He sits behind me in Mrs. Grogan's class. Even worse, he lives next door in the house where Yvonne lived before she moved to Australia.

Is Bert really a monster? You tell me. He looks like one.

He sounds like one.

He acts like one.

He terrifies the Big Pest and Sophie.

He calls me stupid names.

My mom told me to ignore him, so I am. I'm not going to draw any more pictures of Bert. I've already drawn too many.

I drew that one of him on top of the world, and now the whole class thinks he's some kind of hero. Do you think that made Bert any nicer?

No, it made things worse, because now he wants me to draw pictures of him all the time. I'm turning into a monster myself just thinking about him.

My dad said if you can't ignore him, make him laugh. Are you laughing, Bert? This is a picture of you falling in a black hole while Einstein and I soar across the universe.

I WISH!

Chapter 3

STAR MATES!

This is not an I WISH picture! It's an artist's conception!

Einstein told me that since no one can really see a black hole, artists make up what it looks like, just like I did!

Well, almost like I did.

Here's my new artist's conception. See? No holes, and no Bert, just a squished star.

I LOVE being the almost-friend of the smartest girl in the Universe. Especially today!

Good news, Explorers! Tomorrow is the Top Ten Geography Star Search! It's your chance to shine!

It's my chance to shine! Because guess who asked me to be on her team for the Top Ten Geography Star Search contest?

Yes! Judith Einstein and me, Star Mates! Just like my picture! We are sure to win!

Here we are, flying 24,901 miles around the world!

Here we are landing in
ANTARCTICA

Dancing with penguins would be fun if it wasn't freezing! *Brrrr!* Why do they call it Antarctica if it's too cold for ants?

It's too cold for me!

Antarctica is cold, Bea! So let's go from the home of penguins to the home of wombats, koalas, and kangaroos! Let's go to...

Here's Einstein smiling at me because I answered correctly!

Well, almost correctly.

Here's Bert, trying to ruin everything. You can't see him because I'm not going to draw him, but you can hear him.

No way, Bert. I'm not drawing you, especially not in Australia.

I'm only drawing Einstein and Yvonne and me and Yvonne's pet kangaroo and . . .

And a crocodile?

Are there crocodiles in Australia? Crocodiles who look like Bert! No! I'm not going to draw Bert!

Here I am, trying to erase my picture of Bert the crocodile.

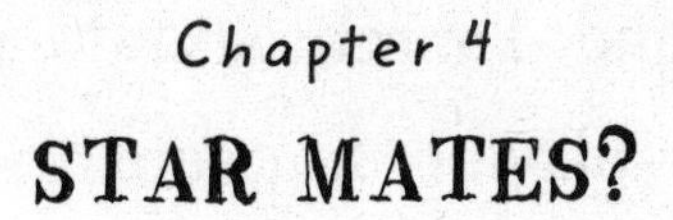

Chapter 4
STAR MATES?

Here I am on the playground with my book and pencil hidden under my shirt. I'm looking for Einstein, my Star Mate!

Keisha and Lauren and Megan and Tristan are playing foursquare. Tommy and Trevon and Maria and Grace are playing basketball.

Ben, Jacob, Fatima, Adelaide, and Lucy are playing monster tag with Bert who is IT, of course. He's growling at the edge of the picture.

Here's Einstein by herself, reading.

There are 6,899 possible questions that could be asked on the Top Ten Geography Star Search, and I only know 67% of the answers.
I thought you knew everything.
6,899 TOP TEN FACTS

Einstein looked at me like I didn't know anything.

I couldn't believe my ears. Einstein was smarter than everybody. She was certain to win. And that meant I was going to win, too!

Einstein didn't answer that question.

Why would Einstein need my help? She knew thousands of answers.

What did I know?

Einstein smiled at my picture. Then she frowned. She didn't look at me.

She looked at Yvonne.

Who is that?
That's my best friend, Yvonne.
You have a best friend?
Yvonne is my first and always best friend, but . . .
Always?
But she moved 10,000 miles away . . .
9,903 to be accurate.
So now you're my almost best friend!

There, I said it. Best friends, almost. Einstein and me. But Einstein just said:

Imaginative and almost accurate, Beatrice.

Then she grabbed my book, crossed out 10,000, and wrote 9,903. In MY book.

I didn't know what to think. I liked my book the way it was.

But I wanted to be Einstein's teammate.

Can I do it? That's what I was wondering when the bell rang.

I looked at #1 on Einstein's list. *What is the longest river in the world?*

I can do it! I already know two answers! The Nile River and Australia! Now I just have to study! I have to study every minute between now and tomorrow and learn 255 more answers. I can stay up all night studying. I HAVE to do it! I have to do it or else.

Or else here I am, falling into an artist's conception of a squished star.

Chapter 5

EINSTEIN'S PENCIL, PART ONE

I can do it! Here I am after recess. I put my book away in my desk. I have my pencil out. I'm ready to write correct answers!

I can do it! I'm writing the correct answer to Question #1. I can do it. Right?

Wrong. Yes, it's me growling, not Bert. I'm growling because the answer that I just wrote is wrong. Here I am erasing my wrong answer and writing the right answer. No, wait.

Here I am erasing my wrong answer and writing the right answer again. And again. And again.

My pencil may have been sharp enough, but my eraser was rubbed out because I'd already erased three wrong answers.

I peeked over at Einstein. All of the correct answers just flowed like a river out of her brain, through her pencil, and onto the paper.

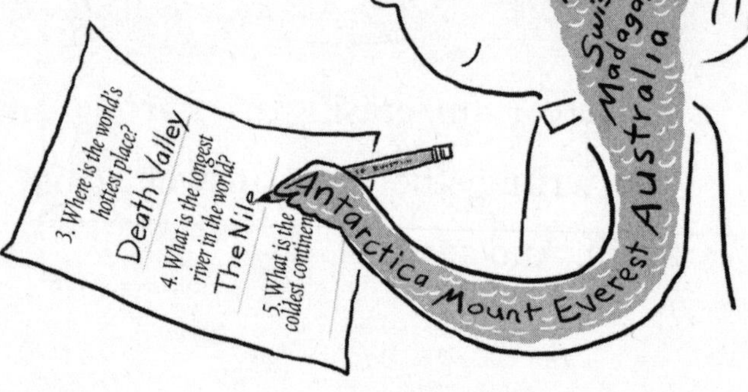

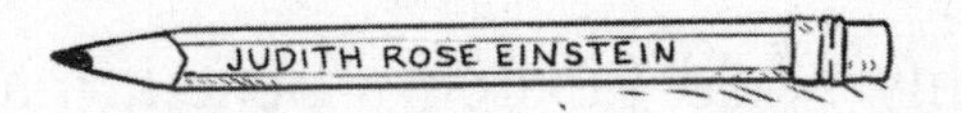

See how her pencil is sharp and the eraser is brand new?

Not like mine.

Her pencil writes correct answers.

My pencil writes wrong answers.

If only I had Einstein's pencil, maybe answers would flow like a river out of my brain, too. I WISH!

Wouldn't that be fun? Complete, correct answers from me, Bea Garcia! I would be the second smartest girl in the universe!

I would write all the correct answers to the ten-minute Quick Quiz just like my Star Mate, Judith Einstein!

Instead, I'm drawing funny pictures like this one. Here we are, sailing Einstein's pencil on the Nile, the longest river in the world.

That's when it hit me like a ton of bricks. I did know the correct answer to Question #1. I had just drawn a picture of it.

If only Mrs. Grogan thinks my pencil is still magic. If funny pictures count, then at least I would get one correct answer.

If only I had Einstein's pencil, I would get them all.

Chapter 6

IT'S NOT STEALING

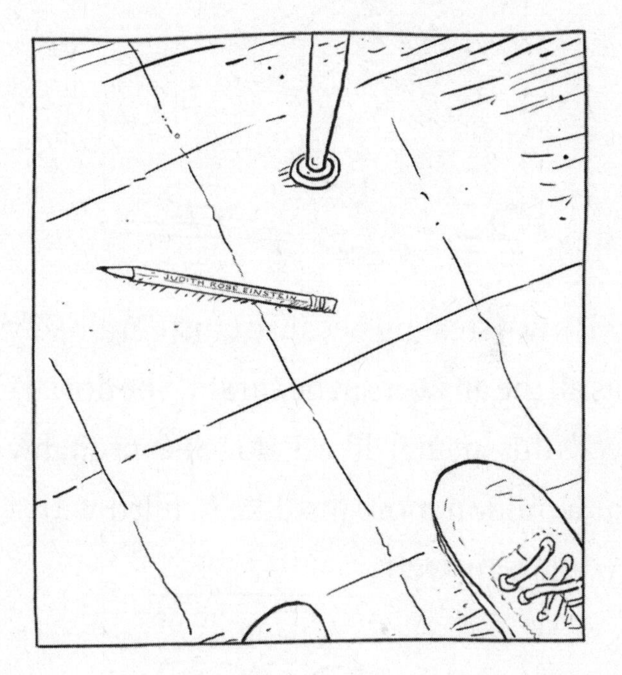

It's not stealing. It's not stealing, if I found Einstein's pencil on the floor after it rolled off her desk.

It's not stealing even if I helped it an eensy-teensy bit by bumping her desk.

It's not stealing because Einstein already has all the answers in her brain. She doesn't need this pencil like I do. She probably has a million more just like it, filled with a gazillion answers.

It's not stealing, it's borrowing. I just need it to study tonight and then I'll give it back right after we win. Nobody saw me pick it up, did they?

Draw me, Buzzy.
Quiet, Bert!

It's not stealing. It's trading. See? I gave my old pencil to Einstein. She said she wanted to learn how to draw like me.

JUDITH

Chapter 7

IT WORKS!

I really truly CAN do it. Here we are on the bus going home. Einstein is quizzing me, and I know the correct answer! Because I have Einstein's pencil in my hand!

No funny pictures, just correct answers!

Just Einstein and me, smiling like new best friends!

Just Einstein and me and the Big Pest.

Just Einstein and me and the Big Pest and Bert.

Bert ruins EVERYTHING! Did he see me take Einstein's pencil?

It doesn't matter. I'm never, never, NEVER going to draw Bert again. No matter what.

I'm just going to close my eyes and ignore Bert until he gets sucked up into the biggest black hole in the universe and nobody ever sees him again.

That was the question Einstein didn't answer before.

I never imagined Einstein with anything like a sister. Or a mother or father. I just imagined her as a human encyclopedia.

Yes. Janet Carol Einstein. She's six years older than me so she thinks she's six years smarter, too. Janet scored a perfect 200 points on the Top Ten Geography Star Search, the best score in history.

Or else I won't be the smartest girl in the school like my sister was.

I tried to imagine someone smarter than Einstein.

How could I help Einstein?

I dragged the Big Pest home. I had work to do. Luckily I had Einstein's pencil.

Chapter 8

IT REALLY WORKS!

Here I am dancing around the kitchen in my Top Ten Geography Star outfit! I know Einstein's pencil will work! I'm going to be a STAR! We're going to win!

Just kidding! I'd never wear that much glitter to school! But here I really am at the kitchen table, writing the correct answer to Question #2 with Einstein's pencil!

And here I am, flying Einstein's pencil 9,903 miles per hour so I can play with Yvonne and her pet kangaroo and still be home in time for dinner. I WISH!

Here's the Big Pest eating crackers with peanut butter and jelly. You can't see him because he's covered in peanut butter and crumbs.

And here's my mom.

Bea, please take out the trash.
She thinks Sophie will take it out for her.

That's not what I'm thinking. It's what I'm WISHING.

Here's Sophie picking up the trash bag, pushing it out the doggy door, and scooting across the garage, around the van, lawn mower, and three bicycles over to the garbage can, where she puts the bag down, tips off the lid, picks up the bag again, jumps three feet up, and lets the bag drop neat as a pin into the garbage can.

Then Sophie skedaddles back to me, her eyes full of LOVE for me, her master and best friend!

I WISH!

And don't forget to put the lid on the garbage can.

Instead, here I am, taking out the trash.

And when I get back, here's my grubby little brother with Einstein's pencil in his peanut-buttery hand drawing in MY book! NO WAY!!!

Here's the monster pest, running away with my pencil!

He was wrong. I caught him.

I grabbed Einstein's pencil by its perfect eraser end . . .

and pulled back . . .

the Big Pest jumped forward and . . .

CRA

Einstein's perfect
pencil broke in two.

I looked at the half of the pencil in my hand. The eraser half. Correct answers were gushing out of the broken pencil. Correct answers that I needed! NO!

The Big Pest looked at me like I was a monster from another planet.

Here's why. I looked like a monster from another planet.

The Big Pest dropped his half of the pencil and ran, faster than fear . . .

out of the house and . . .

up into the crabapple tree in the backyard.

Sophie looked at me like I was a monster from another planet, too.

Then she skedaddled out of the house after the Big Pest.

Scaredy-dog!
Beatrice Garcia! Go to your room!

I grabbed the other half of Einstein's pencil and ran into the bathroom.

When I looked in the mirror, I almost screamed again. They were right. I looked like a monster.

But I couldn't think about that. I had to put Einstein's pencil back together before all the answers ran out.

Chapter 9
IT'S CURSED!

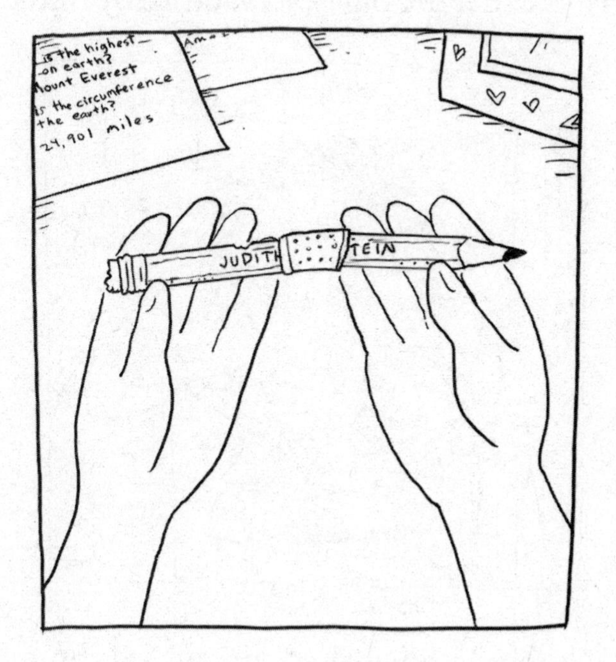

I fixed it. Here's Einstein's pencil. Almost as good as new.

And here I am, in my room where I should be studying for tomorrow's Star Search. Instead I'm carefully erasing the scribble that the Big Pest made in my book.

I know, I know. That's not what I should be doing. I should be writing correct answers, not erasing scribbles. But nobody writes in my book except me.

Then I remembered Einstein. I turned back to the page that she corrected and erased all 9,903 miles of her writing.

When I was done the eraser on Einstein's pencil wasn't perfect anymore. But so what? I wouldn't need an eraser now. I was only going to write correct answers.

Here I am, finally! I'm ready to write all correct answers on a brand-new page.

I already know #1 on Einstein's list.

The longest river in the world is the

It's working! Look! I wrote a clear, correct answer! Almost.

Instead of three straight lines, the letter *N* turned and wiggled . . .

The longest river in the world is the

N

and then so did the *I* and the *L* . . .

The longest river in the world is the

NIL

and the *E*.

The longest river in the world is the

NILE

The longest river in the world is the

NILE

Instead of writing the correct answer with Einstein's pencil I drew this picture of the river Nile.

Here I am, Queen of the Nile, with my pet owl, and my almost best friend, Judith of Egypt, floating 4,180 miles north.

We float past the great pyramids, past golden sands and the mysterious Sphinx.

We see fish, fantastic flowers, strange birds, papyrus reeds, and a crocodile.

A crocodile who looks like Bert.

No! No way! I'm not drawing you, Bert! Not as a crocodile, not as anything!

GRRRRRR!!!
Beat it! Or else!
Bea? Are you all right?
I'm grrrreat, Mom! I'm studying!

I just need to start again. No more funny pictures. Just correct answers. Turn the page, please! Yes, you! Turn the page!

Thank you. I just need to start again on a new page where I will only write correct answers! No pictures! If I don't draw any pictures then I won't draw Bert! Here's the question:

What is the smallest continent?

Can you guess? It starts with an

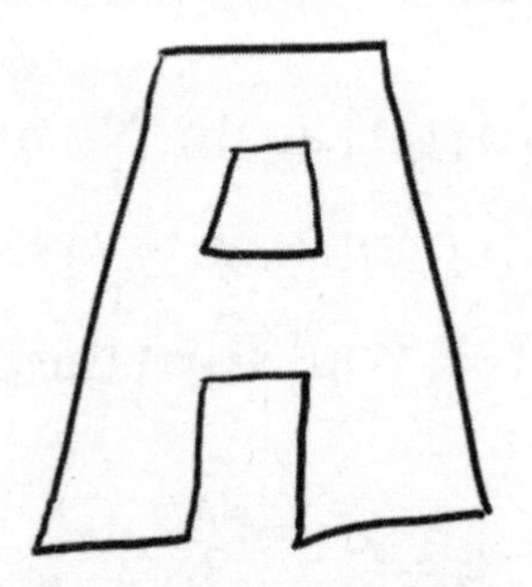

No, it's not Antarctica. It's not Asia, either, or Africa. It's not America, North or South, either. I'll give you another clue.

See how the A is jumping up and down?

And now it's turning into a kangaroo!

Yes! The smallest continent is the only place where kangaroos live! Australia!

Even though it's small, Australia is the only place in the world where you'll find wombats . . .

and koala bears which aren't really bears, and . . .

duck-billed platypuses, which aren't really ducks. Funny, aren't they?

I know I said I wasn't going to draw any funny pictures, but these are really truly animals that only live in Australia.

I know because my best friend, Yvonne, told me.

Here are Yvonne and me playing with Yvonne's pet kangaroo. I know kangaroos don't really play jump rope, but wouldn't it be fun if they did?

Unless they looked like Bert! No! No! No! Get lost, Bert! Beat it! Scram! Get out of my picture!

Here is Yvonne looking at me like I was a monster from another planet.

And here's why. I do look like a monster from another planet.

I'm not a monster! I'm an artist! See? See my pencil?

Come back, Yvonne! I'm not a monster!

I have to stop drawing these pictures!
Help me! Yes, you! Close the book, please!

Wait! Don't close the book!

If you close the book, I'll be caught in these pages like a monster forever!

I wasn't a monster before I took Einstein's pencil. It's the pencil! Einstein's pencil has turned me into a monster! It's cursed! I have to get rid of it and quick!

Bea? Go help Pablo down from the tree.

Chapter 10

KISS THIS CURSED PENCIL GOOD-BYE!

Here is the Big Pest in the crabapple tree, throwing sticks for Sophie down below, who is running around in circles trying to find them.

Here I am, tossing Einstein's pencil as far as I can in the backyard. Which isn't very far. Which is just in front of Sophie, who stops and sniffs.

For the first time in her life Sophie finds a stick that someone throws for her.

Only this time it's not a stick, it's a curse.

Sophie trots to the crabapple tree to give her prize to the Big Pest.

Here she is, her eyes full of LOVE for him, the little rat.

The Big Pest looks at Sophie. Then, for the first time in his life, he gets down from the crabapple tree all by himself and runs into the house.

Sophie trots over to me, drops the cursed Einstein's pencil at my feet, and skedaddles after the Big Pest into the house.

Here it is in the grass at my feet. It looks just like any old broken pencil except it's not. It's cursed.

Here I am, throwing Einstein's pencil as far as I can again.

Which—for once in my life—is far. Here it is sailing high over the fence into another galaxy. I WISH!

Here it is really, sailing high over the fence into Bert's yard. Which may as well be another galaxy because I'm never going to go there so I will never see Einstein's pencil again.

I'm free! I'm free of the curse of Einstein's pencil! Now all I have to do is figure out how to win the Star Search tomorrow without it.

Chapter 11

THE WORST TOMORROW EVER

Here I am, staring at the fake stars on my ceiling. Maybe if I stay awake all night, tomorrow won't even come.

Tomorrow was supposed to be the best day of my life, the day I became a Top Ten Geography Star with my new best friend, Judith Einstein.

Instead it's going to be even worse than the day Yvonne moved to Australia. It's going to be the day I fall into a black hole because I don't have the answers. What could be worse?

Sophie knows I'm not a monster.

Chapter 12

THE EMILY DICKINSON TOP TEN GEOGRAPHY STAR SEARCH

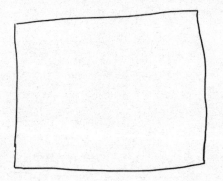

It's already tomorrow and I'm as sick to my stomach as you can be without really being sick. There's no picture because I'm not going to draw myself sick. In fact, I'm not going to draw ANYTHING ever again. Drawing turns me into a monster.

You'll have to imagine me riding the bus to school. In silence.

Imagine me sitting with the Big Pest, who won't talk to me even though I apologized 6,899 times for acting like a monster.

Imagine me sitting with my teammate, Einstein, who looked at me once with her *or else* look and then disappeared into her book of 6,899 Top Ten Geography Facts.

I should say almost silence. Because guess who is still talking?

Draw me, Buzzy Bea.

I don't have a pencil.

Now imagine us in Mrs. Grogan's class.

Good morning, Explorers! Today is your day to shine, the day of the Emily Dickinson Top Ten Geography Star Search! Get a pencil and line up with your teammate!

Draw me, Buzzy Bea.

I don't have a pencil.

Imagine us lining up to go to the cafeteria where . . .

Draw me, Buzzy Bea.

I don't have a pencil.

I am sitting next to my teammate, Einstein, who still hasn't said a word to me. Guess who was right behind me?

Draw me, Buzzy Bea.
I don't have a pencil.

Imagine Mrs. Grogan explaining everything to everybody.

Welcome, Explorers! The envelope in front of you contains ten questions, each on a separate piece of paper like this.
1. Where is the coldest place on earth?
Working with your teammate, write the answer to each question as completely as possible on the lines above the box. Each written answer is worth up to ten points. You may then draw a picture in the box to score up to 100 additional points for a maximum of 200 points. Put each answer back in the envelope as you finish. Is everybody ready?

No, I wasn't ready.

Draw me, Buzzy Bea.

I don't have a pencil.

Use this pencil, Beatrice.

Then Einstein handed me my pencil, the one I left for her when I stole hers. The magic one with no eraser left.

I have another one.

Einstein showed me her pencil. It was a brand-new one with her name on it. I was right. She did have a million of those.

You have thirty minutes exactly to answer all ten questions.

I write, you draw.
Ready, Beatrice?

No, I wasn't ready. But Einstein was already writing the answer to *Question #1: Where is the coldest place on Earth?*

Einstein can't win without me? I used my magic pencil.

I drew Bert in the coldest place on Earth.

I drew Bert baking in Death Valley.

I drew him climbing to the highest point on Earth on top of Mount Everest and . . .

diving to the lowest point on Earth at the bottom of the Pacific Ocean.

I drew Bert swinging through the Amazon rain forest . . .

skiing in the Alps . . .

and flying 24,901 miles around the world.

I even drew Bert jumping with Yvonne and her pet kangaroo in Australia and floating on the river Nile.

I was almost done. I had drawn nine pictures and they were all correct, thanks to Einstein. AND they were funny thanks to Bert. There was one more question for Einstein to answer, one more picture for me to draw.

Question #10: Where is your home?

Einstein wrote a complete, correct answer.

My home is located at 38.9514° North and 92.3283° West on the continent of North America, in the country of the United States, in the state of Missouri.

And then it was my turn.

Draw me, Buzzy Bea! Please, please draw me!

Draw Bert? At my house? No way! I don't care if he said double please.

Quickly, Beatrice, we're running out of time! It's up to you!

I drew Bert. Turn the page, you'll see.

Chapter 13

WE ARE STARS!

Here we are in the crabapple tree in my backyard. Einstein and me.

And Bert.

Einstein didn't mean that we were movie stars. She didn't even mean we were Top Ten Geography Stars.

She meant we were really, truly stars. The kind that really shine and are so far away we can't even measure the distance in regular miles.

We got down from the tree, and I drew Einstein a picture of the universe with this pencil.

They gave us both ten of these pencils for winning the Star Search with a maximum score of 200 points + 60 points more for creativity. That was 60 points more than Einstein's sister scored.

And thanks to Bert, too, in a funny weird way. But don't tell him I said that.

Einstein and I also got globes that actually spin like the real Earth. Now I don't need to fly 9,802 miles per hour to get to Australia where Einstein told me there really are wild crocodiles, but not where Yvonne lives.

We are stars. Even Bert, but I'm only saying that to be accurate, because Einstein said it was true. To me, he's still a monster.

sorry. I'm sorry. I'm sorry. I'm sorry. I'm sorry. I'm sorry.I'm sor
sorry.I'm sorry. I'm sorry. I'm sorry. I'm sorry. I'm sorry. I'm sorr
sorry.I'm sorry. I'm sorry. I'm sorry. I'm sorry. I'm sorry.I'm sorr
sorry.I'm sorry. I'm sorry. I'm sorry. I'm sorry. I'm sorry. I'm sor
sorry.I'm sorry. I'm sorry. I'm sorry. I'm sorry. I'm sorry. I'm sor
sorry.I'm sorry. I'm sorry. I'm sorry. I'm sorry. I'm sorry. I'm sor
sorry.I'm sorry. I'm sorry. I'm sorry. I'm sorry. I'm sorry. I'm sor
sorry.I'm sorry. I'm sorry. I'm sorry. I'm sorry. I'm sorry. I'm sor
n sorry.I'm sorry. I'm sorry. I'm sorry. I'm sorry. I'm sorry. I'm sorr
n sorry. I'm sorry. I'm sorry. I'm sorry. I'm sorry. I'm sorry.I'm sorr
m sorry. I'm sorry. I'm sorry. I'm sorry. I'm sorry.I'm sorry.I'm sorry
'm sorry. I'm sorry. I'm sorry. I'm sorry. I'm sorry. I'm sorry. I'm sorry.
I'm sorry.I'm sorry.I'm sorry. I'm sorry. I'm sorry. I'm sorry. I'm sorry.
I'm sorry.I'm sorry. I'm sorry I'm sorry. I'm sorry. I'm sorry.
I'm sorry.I'm sorry. I'm sorry. I'm sorry. I'm sorry. I'm sorry.
I'm sorry. I'm sorry. I'm sorry. I'm sorry. I'm sorry.
I'm sorry. I'm sorry. I'm sorry.

I apologized 6,899 more times to the Big Pest for acting like a monster. I think saying *I'm sorry* ten times should have been enough, especially since I meant it. But it wasn't, so I made him a pencil with stars and his real name.

Even then the Big Pest wouldn't forgive me until I let him draw a picture in my book. Here it is. It's either a frog or a monster, you decide.

But that's the only picture he'll ever draw in my book. He can get his own book and keep his peanut-buttery fingers off of mine.

MONSTER
SCRIBBLES
by THE
BIG PEST

Draw me, Buzzy!

I'm never drawing Bert again, no matter what. He still calls me Buzzy.

Besides, Bert's got a pencil. He can draw his own pictures.

NO! Bert had Einstein's pencil! Even though I knew it wasn't really truly cursed, I couldn't take any chances. What if it turned him into more of a monster than he already was?

I grabbed Einstein's pencil. Then I threw it as far as I could into another galaxy.

Sophie jumped high, high into the air . . .

and caught it.

Here we all are, soaring across the universe. Even Bert. Wait, watch out, Bert! Don't fall into that artist's conception of a black hole! Oops.

Just kidding! Here we are really, soaring across the universe in the picture I painted on the fence between Bert's yard and mine.

Einstein and the Big Pest and Sophie helped. Everybody helped, even Bert. He was an inspiration.

This last page is just me, Bea Garcia. It's okay to close the book now. I won't be caught in here like a monster forever. Because I am a star, really truly.

Just like you.

This is Bert, the monster next door.

This is his new pet, Big Kitty.

This is Sophie, the world's smartest dog.

But not the bravest.

Find out what happens when my scaredy-dog meets Bert's monster cat in the next Bea Garcia book.

Tale of Scaredy-Dog

Coming in 2018